Other Books By
Mike Neigoff

Best in Camp
Dive In!
Free Throw
Goal to Go
Nine Make a Team
Smiley Sherman, Substitute
Two on First
Up Sails

Mike Neigoff

hal, tennis champ

Pictures by Fred Irvin

ALBERT WHITMAN & Company   **Chicago**

CONTENTS

1 Challenge to the Champion

The sun was in his eyes as Hal rushed the net, his eyes slitted so he saw only the tennis ball. He knew the exact spot he wanted to be at and he reached the spot, never taking his eye from the ball.

He had a fraction of a second to get set and hit the ball. His heart was pounding inside his chest, but no one could tell. Hal looked calm as he lifted his racket and used all his power to smash the ball into the right court.

On the other side of the net, Tedson raced from the left side of the backcourt to reach the ball. It was hopeless. He couldn't reach the ball.

"Deuce!" Hal cried. He felt good. He wiped the sweat from his face with the back of his hand. Deuce meant the game was tied up. To win, one of the players had to make two points in a row.

"Deuce-smoosh, so long as you tied up the game, you're happy," Tedson said, panting for breath.

"That's right," Hal said. He did not joke about tennis. He was already in position, knees bent, right hand holding the racket. With his left hand he cradled the racket at the throat, the part next to the strings.

"Your serve," Hal called.

"OK," Tedson said. "I don't know why I keep trying. You never let me win. Are you ready?"

"Ready," Hal said, and he tensed a bit. It was only a game played for fun, but he had to win. He couldn't lose. Even against his best friend he had to win!

Tedson served. Hal let the ball bounce and then his racket met it squarely and the ball lifted over the net. Tedson rushed forward and stroked the ball before it could bounce. Hal backpedaled, let the ball bounce, and then smashed it back.

Tedson was ready this time, and he returned the ball. They had a rally going, hitting the ball back and forth over the net. The rally continued at a fast, hard pace until Ted drove the ball into the net.

"My advantage!" Hal cried. He was breathing hard. Advantage was the first of the two winning points he had to make in a row. He needed another point now to win the game.

"I know, I know!" Tedson sighed. "But maybe, just maybe, it will be deuce again."

"Not this time," Hal said. Tedson was his best friend and he was a good tennis player, but Hal knew he was going to take the next point and win the game.

"The sky wouldn't come crashing down if

I won just one game," Tedson said, walking back to the baseline. "I mean, you have won five straight games from me this afternoon. Your record won't be hurt by letting me win this one."

Hal smiled. Tedson was joking as usual. He didn't mind losing to Hal. It didn't make any difference to him if he won or lost. It did to Hal.

"Quit clowning and serve!" Hal said.

Tedson served and Hal took a slice at the ball so that it touched the top of the net and then went dribbling along the ground.

"My game!" Hal cried.

"Wow! That was sneaky," Tedson said, coming up to the net. "You have to teach me that slice so I can be sneaky, too."

"I'll be glad to help you practice the shot," Hal said. He grinned. He felt good. "You played at the top of your form today, Tedson. You made me work to win. If you'd work out afternoons, you could be a really hot tennis player."

They walked toward the bench, and Tedson waved to a tall, dark-haired boy who had been watching them play.

"Coming from you, that's high praise," Tedson said. He smiled, and he wasn't kidding now. "Thanks. I thought I played rather well today."

"Good shot!" the boy said as they came up to the bench.

"Hi, Tony," Tedson said. "Hal, the boy tennis champion, always makes fantastic shots like that."

"I believe it," Tony said. "When are you and I going to play a set, Hal?"

Hal didn't want to answer so he sat on the bench and carefully put his racket in the press.

"I wish someone else had to take the beatings I take from him on the tennis court," Tedson said.

Hal looked at Tedson and smiled. Tedson understood Hal didn't want to answer Tony's question.

Tedson put on his comic-sad face and turned to Tony. "You just don't know what it means to lose to Hal all the time," he said. "I have to sneak into the house and tell my poor mother and my poor father that I am a failure on the tennis courts."

Hal grinned. Ted was funny when he began his long story of complaints.

"The shame of it all!" Ted wailed, slapping his forehead. "My father, Theodore Buris, has given me his proud name and allows me to be known to the world as Ted-son, son of Ted. My proud father must hang his head in public because of the disgrace I bring to his name by losing to Hal all the time."

Tony laughed. "You're a nut, Tedson." Then he turned to Hal.

"How about a game?"

"I'm worn out from playing Tedson," Hal said. "And I have to get home for lunch."

"We could play tomorrow," Tony said. He wasn't letting Hal off that easy.

Hal couldn't get out of answering the

question. He didn't want to hurt Tony's feelings, but he didn't want to play him.

"You don't want to play me," Hal said. "You're still a beginner at tennis. You only began playing last year."

Tony nodded. "I know. You're the big tennis champ around here, but I think I can take you!"

Tedson tried to make a joke of the situation.

"You know, Tony," he said, "it isn't polite to challenge the tennis champ. You wait until he asks you to play him."

"Is that so?" Tony asked, and his words bristled. He was angry. Hal was getting angry in return. Who did this beginner think he was to demand that he play him?

"Don't get mad," Tedson said. "Hal will play you one of these days."

"He's going to play me a lot sooner than he thinks," Tony said. "I talked to Coach Milt Cohen and there's going to be a tournament for kids our age. I'm signed up."

14

Turning to Hal, Tony said, "If you're really a champion, you'll have to play me."

"That's right," Tedson said. "I heard something about a tournament for sub-juniors."

"I didn't know Coach Cohen would let beginners play in a tournament," Hal said.

"Are you afraid a beginner might beat you?" Tony asked.

"Hal doesn't have to worry about anyone beating him," Tedson said. "He never loses. His father has been coaching him for years. He's going to be a pro. He doesn't lose."

"I don't know if I'll enter the tournament," Hal said slowly. He didn't want to have Tony angry at him. Tony kept thinking Hal was trying to insult him. He just didn't understand Hal wouldn't get any fun out of playing a game against a beginner.

"I don't know if I'll sign up either," Tedson said. "I have a photography assignment for the camera club. And so do you, Hal."

"I've entered," Tony said. "And I have weekly practice with the school band, and

15

I have my assignments for the school newspaper. But I'll play in the tournament."

"If you can find time, I can too," said Tedson. "I'll sign up."

Tony looked at Hal. "If you don't enter the tournament, you'll be saying you're afraid to play me."

"I'm not afraid of beginners," Hal said. "I'll sign up, and I'll win. You'll be lucky if you even get to play against me in one of the early rounds."

"I'll play you," Tony said, "and I'll win!"

He walked away and Hal stared after him.

"There is one angry fellow," Tedson said.

"I didn't mean to get him angry," Hal said. "But there's no point to my playing him. He's a beginner."

"Well, you don't have to worry about him," Tedson said. "Let's find Coach Cohen and sign up for the tournament."

Hal knew he didn't have to worry about losing to Tony. But he still felt that beginners should not be allowed to play in the tournament. He didn't want to waste a lot of time playing beginners. It was better practice to play advanced players.

Hal wasn't worried about winning the tournament. He always won. He knew that, sometime, everyone lost—and he supposed that could happen to him, too. But he didn't want to think about it.

2 Follow Through

Hal's mother was on her knees in the garden when he came home. She was working with a trowel.

She wiped her hands on her slacks as Hal came up the walk.

"Did you have a good game, Hal?" she asked.

"I just played Tedson," Hal said. "He's getting better all the time. I really had to work a couple of times to win."

"Ted only plays the game for fun," his mother said. "I'm glad the weather has lost its chill so I can get the garden ready for

18

planting. I was not happy with the way the roses turned out last summer."

"What was wrong with them?" Hal asked. "They looked all right to me."

His mother laughed. "I doubt if you or your father even noticed that we had roses. We could have weeds shoulder high and you two would never blink an eye."

"That's not fair," Hal said. "We know the difference between roses and weeds."

"Good, then you won't mind raking up the dead grass for me," his mother said.

Hal groaned. "I was thinking of getting in some tennis this afternoon," he said.

"But you played tennis this morning," his sister Julie said from the steps of the house. She had her hair up in curlers, and Hal thought she looked silly.

"I have to get in some practice," Hal said. "There's going to be a park tournament. Why don't you sign up?"

"I have more important things to do than play tennis," she said.

19

"More important things?" Hal asked in wonder. "What's so important? All you ever do is keep changing the style of your hair."

"That's important to a girl," Mrs. Brock said. "And Julie doesn't change her hairdo that often."

"You really ought to find out if there's going to be a girls' division in the tournament," Hal told Julie. "You're a good tennis player."

"Thanks," Julie said, "but no thanks. If I entered the tournament, Dad would be after me to train and work and study tennis. He still dreams I could be the woman singles champ. Two summers ago he kept me so busy with tennis that I didn't get a chance to do anything else."

Their mother laughed. "I remember that summer," she said. "I thought I was housemother to a tennis club. There was tennis talk at every meal and tennis all day long and tennis books in the evening. Frankly, I have had my fill of tennis."

"Dad hasn't," said Julie. "Now he is giving

Hal the treatment. Hal is going to be our next champion."

"Dad thinks I can make it," Hal said seriously. "I don't mind the training."

Hal's mother looked at him. She said, "If all that tennis begins to choke you, don't be afraid to tell your father that you want out."

"I couldn't do that!" Hal said. "Dad wouldn't understand. Tennis is important to him, and to me, too!"

Mrs. Brock sighed. "I don't mind at all that your father is a tennis nut," she said. "But don't let him make you one, unless that's what you really want."

Picking up the trowel, she added, "It would be nice to have a man around the house who notices that the front yard has flowers and not tomatoes growing in it."

Hal laughed. "We know the difference between roses and tomatoes," he said. "You can't eat roses. I'm going to shower. I worked up a sweat on the courts."

After lunch, Hal walked over to the business district and the store with "Bo Brock Sports" written across the glass pane.

Hal's father was waiting on a man who was looking at golf balls.

Hal wandered over to the tennis section to see if the new rackets had arrived. Behind the counter there were pictures on the wall of Hal's dad wearing white tennis shorts and a v-neck white sweater, a tennis racket in his hand. He was standing next to the tennis champion. There were trophies behind the counter, too. They had been won by Bo Brock when he was in college. There were pictures of the whole family, all with tennis rackets.

With the pictures was a framed copy of the newspaper story of two years ago when Hal had won the peewee tournament at the park.

The customer left, and Hal's father put the golf balls away.

"You ought to take down that old newspaper clipping," Hal said. "You don't have to be very good to win the peewee tournament."

"You have to be good enough to beat the competition," Bo Brock said. "You did that. I'll take it down when I can put up a story about how you won the National Clay-courts."

Hal squirmed. He didn't like this kind of talk. It was as though his father praised him in front of his teacher. It was uncomfortable.

He looked at his dad. Bo Brock was tall and lean. There was no fat on him. He had some gray hairs, but he looked younger than the fathers of any of the boys Hal knew.

"How can you be so sure I'll win?" Hal asked.

His father picked up a tennis ball from the counter and bounced it on the floor.

"Training," he said. "You have a good body and a good mind and all you need is good coaching. I've been providing that since you were old enough to hold a tennis racket."

"You make it sound easy," said Hal.

His father squeezed the tennis ball and smiled. "No one said it was easy. To be a champion, you have to have a strong desire. You have to want to win more than anything in the whole world."

Hal nodded. "But everyone wants to win."

"You have to want it more than everyone else," his father said. He smiled. "Your mother and everyone else think I'm a tennis nut. You have to be if you want to be champion. You need a single-track mind. You have to play tennis, study tennis, think tennis, and even dream tennis."

Mr. Brock looked at Hal. "I know what I'm talking about. I could have made it when I was in college, but I broke my ankle and then I met your mother and I wanted other things besides tennis."

Hal smiled. "I'm glad you did."

"But you can do it," his father said. "If you want it badly enough."

Hal was thinking about what his father

had said when the door of the shop opened. Hal looked up and saw Tony Scott heading for the tennis section.

Hal frowned. What did he want?

"I'm looking for a new racket," Tony said. He grinned at Hal's father. "Do you mind selling me a good racket so I can beat Hal in the park tournament?"

Bo Brock laughed, but Hal didn't think it was funny. Tony had a lot of nerve!

"I'll sell you the best racket in the store," Mr. Brock said.

"Don't expect miracles," Hal said, smiling. "It's only a tennis racket. I'm going to win. But we'll sell you a good racket so you won't have any excuses about poor equipment when I beat you."

"Try this racket and see how it feels in your hand," Mr. Brock said, handing Tony a racket. "It's our best racket. It has gut strings. They cost more than nylon and wear out sooner, but are worth the extra cost."

"That's interesting," said Tony. "I haven't

paid much attention to equipment. I haven't been playing long, at least the way I guess you'd look at it. In fact," and he grinned, "Hal thinks I'm a beginner."

"It's never too early to learn about equipment," Mr. Brock said. "Most champions use a gut-strung racket. If you're going to be a first-class player, you should read up on equipment."

"I've just been playing for fun," Tony said. "But I play in the band for fun, too, and I notice that I play better since I bought a good clarinet."

"You have to practice to play in the band," Mr. Brock said. "Where are you going to get the time to become a good tennis player?"

"Maybe Tony doesn't have to work hard to become good at tennis," Hal said. "He's a whiz at about everything he does. It all comes easy to him."

"That's right," Tony said, "it does come easy. I guess I have natural talent. I play in the band. I'm on the newspaper staff. I'm a member of the history club, and I think I'll join the photography club. You're a member, aren't you, Hal?"

Hal nodded. "You can join the camera club," he said. "We take beginners there."

Bo Brock laughed. He was still thinking about tennis. "Competition makes a tournament more interesting," he said.

"I'll take this racket," Tony said. "I see it's the same kind Hal uses. I like the idea of you selling me the racket I'll use to win over Hal."

Was Tony serious or joking? Hal couldn't decide.

"It's a good racket," Mr. Brock said, "but I can't guarantee you'll win with it."

Hal watched silently as his father made out a receipt and rang up the sale. Tony grinned and waved as he left the shop.

Hal's father said, "He may be a beginner, but he sounds very sure of himself."

Hal nodded. He wondered if he should tell his father Tony just didn't understand about tennis. Tony could not see anything wrong with challenging a better player to a game. Hal thought anyone ought to know better than that.

Tony was making it a personal fight and seemed to be enjoying it. Hal would just have to teach him a lesson!

3 Advantage for Tony

The next morning, Miss French, the English teacher, asked Hal to remain after class. He tried to guess what she wanted to talk to him about, and he was worried. He hadn't given her any trouble and while his marks weren't tops, they were not bad enough for her to have to warn him about failing.

As soon as the class cleared out of the door, Miss French handed Hal back his last theme.

"I want you to write another theme, Hal," she said. "I could give you a passing grade on this one, but it is almost the same as the last theme you wrote."

"Oh, the two themes are very different, Miss French," Hal said. He was surprised anyone would think the two papers were alike.

"This one is about a tennis match a friend and I played," Hal said. "The other theme was about the United States open tennis championship matches. They are entirely different!"

Miss French smiled. She had a nice smile, but it didn't make Hal feel any better. He did not want to write an extra theme.

"One tennis game reads very much like another to me," Miss French said. "I get very confused by all the mentions of lobs, overhand smashes, and net play. I'm afraid, Hal, that I'm just not a tennis fan."

"You said we could write about anything we wanted to," Hal said.

"Yes, I know I did," Miss French said. "But every single paper you have written

31

has been about tennis. There have to be other things in which you're interested and could write about."

Hal shrugged. He was interested in other things, but he knew tennis best. In fact, tennis was the only thing he was good at. He wasn't like Tony who was good at a lot of things.

"There's plenty to say about tennis," Hal told Miss French. "A lot of books have been written about the game."

"I'm sure they have," Miss French said. "But I am going to insist that you write about something else. You can do that, can't you?"

"I'll try," Hal said. "But tennis is what I like best."

Miss French smiled. "Learn about other things. You'll find that the more you know about a subject, the more fun it is."

Hal didn't think that was fair, but she was the teacher and he would have to do as she said. He could write about photography, but Tedson knew more about it than he did.

At lunch Hal told Tedson about what had happened and his friend laughed.

Hal looked at him. It wasn't funny at all.

"Did you really write paper after paper about different tennis matches?" Tedson asked.

"Of course," Hal said. "What is so strange about that?"

"You're boring her," Tedson said. "It may come as a shock to you, Hal, but not everyone cares that much about tennis."

Hal smiled. "Well," he said, "I suppose if you don't know anything about tennis, a theme about a match could sound kind of odd. But tennis is all I really know. What else can I write about?"

"Write about the camera club," Tedson suggested. "There's a meeting after school. You're coming to it, aren't you?"

"I thought I'd get in a little time on the courts," Hal said. "I want to be ready for the tournament."

"You're a lot better than everyone else

already," Tedson said. "You don't need that extra practice. Come to the camera club meeting and you'll have something you can write about for your theme."

"All right," said Hal. "I guess I have to. Miss French wants that theme turned in by the end of the week."

"Miss French is nice," Tedson said with a glint in his eye and his lips curling into a smile. "Now, if we only had a teacher who taught French and her name was Miss English, that would be something."

Hal didn't laugh. To Tedson everything was funny, even an English teacher named Miss French. Tedson didn't have Hal's problems. Tedson was very good at English. He could dash off a new theme during lunch period. Hal knew it would take him hours to write something good enough to turn in to the teacher.

The camera club met in a basement room of the school. Part of the room was arranged as a photographic laboratory. Photographic enlargers lined one wall and facing them were worktables and a tank of running water.

Two new students came to the meeting. One was a small blonde girl wearing glasses.

"My uncle gave me his old Speed Graphic camera," she explained, "and I don't know how to use it."

She had brought the camera with her. It was the kind newspaper photographers use.

The club president, Fred Romati, reached for the camera and his eyes almost grew misty with pleasure.

"It's a dandy," he said. "My father has one, and I know how to use it. I'll be glad to show you. I wish I had one like it!"

The other newcomer to the club was Tony Scott.

Hal frowned. When he had told Tony he'd be welcome to join the camera club he hadn't thought Tony would be serious. But here he was. And Hal felt sure Tony already had a prize-winning picture.

"I don't know anything about darkroom work and I'd like to learn," Tony said.

Hal felt better. At least there was one thing Tony Scott couldn't do better than everyone else. Hal smiled as he made a mental correction. Two things. He couldn't play tennis as well as Hal.

Frank welcomed Tony to the club and said, "Tedson will explain how we get a photograph from a negative. If everyone is ready, we'll turn off the overhead lights and turn on the safe lights. Phil, make sure the door is locked so no one can come in and let light into the room to fog our paper."

Tedson took Tony aside and told him he would show him how negatives were made from film and how the negative then was placed in an enlarger. When the light inside the enlarger was turned on, it would shine through the negative onto photographic paper.

Hal listened to Tedson as he placed a negative of his own in the carrier and slipped it

into the enlarger. He snapped on the light, moved the easel below the enlarger into position. He adjusted the bellows until the image was in focus on the easel.

"It's like a slide projector," Tony said. "But instead of showing a picture on a screen, you show it on a piece of paper."

"That's right," Tedson said. "You catch on quick."

"I just happen to be interested in everything," Tony said. "This seems easy. I should

37

be able to make a picture from a negative the way Hal is doing. Nothing to it. Right, Hal?"

"It isn't that easy," Hal said, annoyed. Tony was bragging, and Hal had an idea he was boasting just to make him angry.

"Let's watch Hal expose a piece of paper," Tedson said.

Hal turned off the light, slipped a sheet of photographic paper emulsion side up into the easel. Then he clicked on the light and counted out fifteen seconds before switching off the light.

"The paper is still blank," said Tony.

"That's right," said Hal with an edge to his voice. "You don't know all about photography yet."

"Watch what happens when Hal puts the paper into the tray with the developing solution," Tedson said.

Hal moved over to a table on which three trays were placed. He slipped the paper into the first tray and rocked it gently. The paper swam in the solution, and the three boys watched as very slowly and very dimly at first, a picture began to form on the paper. After a minute or so, the picture was much clearer and darker. It was a picture of Tedson stretching on his toes to hit a tennis ball just over his head.

"That's a good shot," Tedson said.

Hal felt good. That was praise, coming from Tedson. He liked the picture. The camera had caught Tedson at just the second before he hit the ball with his racket.

"It's not a bad picture," Tony said.

Hal bit his lip to keep from saying what he was thinking. He used tongs to slip the picture out of the tray with developing solution and into the stop-action bath. The chemicals stopped the picture from getting too dark. Then, using tongs again, he slipped the photograph into the hypo bath.

"The stop-action bath gets rid of the developing solution," Tedson explained. "The hypo bath sets the picture so it won't fade. In about ten minutes, Hal will put the picture in the wash tank and then all he has to do is dry it."

"It doesn't sound very difficult," Tony said.

"I'd like to see you do it," Hal said.

"There's a lot more to it than just moving the paper from one tray to another," Tedson said. "For example, Hal has a good picture here, but it can be improved. You'll notice my face in the picture is kind of light, chalky looking. It should be dodged in. Do you mind if I borrow the negative and show Tony how to dodge?" Tedson asked.

"No, I don't mind," Hal said. But he did mind. He didn't enjoy having Tony see that Tedson knew more about photography than Hal did. But Hal had to admit that Tedson was much better at darkroom technique than he was. Hal could be as good as Tedson if he studied it more and worked at it, he told himself.

After they had cleaned up their equipment and left the lab in neat order, the boys walked out of the school building.

"That was fun," Tony said. "I'm going to join the club. I'd like to be very good at processing negatives and printing my own pictures."

"But you're already busy with the school band and the newspaper and playing tennis," Hal said.

"Oh, I can do a lot of things at the same time and do pretty well, " Tony said, smiling. "It's easy. What's the matter, Hal, are you afraid of the competition?"

"Of course not," Hal said quickly. "The camera club will take all the members it can get."

"That's right," Tedson said. "Let's go to my house and I'll show you the little darkroom I have."

"I'd like to," Hal said, "but I can't. I have to run home and change clothes and get to the courts so I can work on my game."

Tedson nodded. "You know," he said, "you could get in some practice by playing

Tony. It wouldn't have to be a real game. Just practice."

Tony looked up and nodded. "Yes," he said, "why not?"

Hal bit his lip and did not answer, and Tony laughed as he and Tedson walked away.

4 Dad Knows Best?

Hal raced home and found his father waiting, pacing the living room floor. Bo Brock was dressed for tennis in a white shirt and shorts and new thick-soled tennis shoes. His tennis racket was on the couch.

"Where have you been?" Mr. Brock asked. "I've been waiting for an hour. I asked Jim to take over at the shop so I could help you get in some practice."

"I'm sorry, Dad," Hal said. "I didn't know you were going to be here waiting. I went to a camera club meeting."

"You should have known that I was going to be waiting for you," his father said. He smiled. "I'm your coach, and I want to make sure you win the park tournament."

"I'm probably the only fellow who is practicing today," Hal said. "Tony Scott came to the camera club meeting, and he said he wasn't going to work out on the courts today."

"That's why you're going to win. You take the game seriously," Bo Brock said. "We would have had more time for practice today if you had skipped going to the camera club meeting."

"But I like the camera club," Hal said.

"Let's not talk about it now," his father said hurriedly. "Get changed—we're wasting time."

Hal went to his room to change his clothes. The camera club had taken time he could have used on the tennis court. But he needed the time in the photo lab if he was ever going to be as good as Tedson at printing pictures. And he wanted to be a good photographer.

Hal liked the darkroom work. It was almost magic when the blank piece of paper turned into a photograph as it bobbed about in the developing solution. It was as thrilling as when he drove a tennis ball to the exact spot he wanted it to go.

He liked tennis and photography. He wanted to keep on working at both. He did not want to think that he was going to have to give up one for the other.

By the time Hal had changed into his tennis clothes, his father was outside, waiting in the car.

"We'll work on your backhand today," his father said as he drove to the park.

"That's a good idea," Hal said. "I'm a little weak there."

His father was silent for a moment. Then he said softly, "Hal, do you feel I'm pushing you too hard on tennis?"

"No," said Hal. "I like to work out with

you. I'm lucky to have you for a coach."

"Good. I always wanted to be a tennis champion myself, and that's what I want for you. You do want to be a tennis champion, don't you?"

"Sure," said Hal with a grin. "But I don't want to give up the camera club."

Bo Brock frowned. "I won't make you give up anything. I just don't want to push you into doing something you don't want to do. I always thought you wanted to be a tennis champion more than anything else."

"I do," Hal said quickly.

"But you want to spend time on photography, too. Sometimes you may have to make a choice. If you really want to be a tennis champ, the choice will be easy because nothing else will count. Not many boys want something that much, but for those who do, the prize is worth it. Imagine, out of all the thousands and thousands who play tennis, you could be the one who is better than anyone else. The champion!"

Hal nodded. His father sounded as though he were reciting a prayer.

But Hal worried. Suppose there came a time when he knew he didn't want to be a tennis champion. How could he tell his father?

Mr. Brock parked the car and in a few minutes he and Hal were on the tennis court. They rallied to get warmed up. Bo Brock played a hard game of tennis. He went after every fair ball and gave nothing away. His son played the same kind of game.

"All right," Bo Brock called. "I'll serve them up to your backhand."

Hal took the ready position and used his backhand when the ball came. His father returned the ball to the same place and Hal used his backhand stroke again and again.

His father walked up to the net after one of Hal's shots went out of bounds.

"Your backswing was a bit too high," his father said. "You're beginning to forget what I told you about bending from the knees.

You're bending from the waist. It's a bad habit to get into."

Hal thought about what his father had said and nodded. He hadn't thought about it before, but his father was right.

They worked out more. Hal used only his backhand stroke and every so often his father would suggest an improvement in the way he held the racket, in the position of the elbow during the stroke. They worked on the backhand slice until his father nodded and decided they had practiced enough.

"Time to go," his father said.

They walked off the court and Mr. Brock wiped his face with a towel and then tossed it to Hal who did the same.

"That was a good workout," a voice said from a bench near the fence.

Hal looked up and saw the coach, Milton Cohen.

"How are you, Milt?" Mr. Brock asked. "I hear you're going to play the circuit soon. We'll miss you around here."

The coach smiled. "I'll miss this place, too. I'm in no hurry to leave."

"If I were you, I'd be eager to begin," Hal's father said.

"Me, too," said Hal. "It must be exciting to play all the top players in the country."

Coach Cohen shrugged. "It can get pretty exciting around here, too," he said. "It's exciting when I see a young fellow like you developing into a really top-notch player under the coaching you get from your dad. And it's a thrill to see a boy who has had no real coaching, like Tony Scott, come along with a great natural ability."

Hal frowned. Tony Scott again! He thought Tony was just boasting about how good he was, but here was the coach saying the boy had natural ability.

"You need both," Hal's father said. "I'm counting on the years of training I've given Hal."

"I wish I had had that kind of coaching when I was a young boy," the coach said. "I didn't start playing tennis seriously until I was in college. I had a lot to learn in a short time. Frankly, I'm worried about how good I really am."

"You beat everyone around here," Hal said.

"There isn't much competition around here for me to beat," said the coach. "Will I win when I play the champions? That's the question."

Hal's father nodded. "The only way to find out is to play them," he said.

"You're sure to win," Hal said. He liked the coach.

"I hope so," Coach Cohen said. "I've talked to some friends who are playing the circuit and they tell me it's a hard life. You're on the move all the time. You live out of hotel rooms and don't have a home. You eat in restaurants all the time. And you have to win all the time."

"Of course," said Mr. Brock. "You have to win all the time."

"Sure," said the coach. "Even when you're feeling punk, you have to get out on the courts and win."

Hal had never thought about that. He had imagined it was all championship games and smashing home the set point. He had never thought about the life of the champions when they weren't on the courts.

"Still, it's a great life," Bo Brock said. "I always wanted to try it myself, and Hal is going to know what it feels like to win at Forest Hills and the other places."

"Don't worry," Hal said. "You'll win."

The coach smiled and threw back his shoulders and chuckled. "You're right, Hal," he said. "We have to think about winning. That's what makes a champion."

Hal frowned. It was true that he himself thought a good deal about winning. Right now, he was worrying about the park tournament, and play had not yet begun. But he had not thought of a champion being so worried all the time about winning. Of course if you lost, you were out of the competition.

He didn't want to be afraid all the time that he might lose. Did that mean he didn't want to be a tennis champion?

5 A Fun Game

Hal walked to school the next morning with Tedson. Both boys carried cameras.

Tedson was looking through the view-finder of his twin-lens reflex camera as they walked. Hal's 35-mm. camera was slung over his shoulder.

"I'm going to take pictures all around the school and even in class," said Tedson. "I'm not going to take any posed shots. They're all going to be candids."

"You must have hundreds of pictures

you've made of the outside and inside of the school," said Hal.

Tedson nodded and snapped the view-finder shut into place. "There are some scenes I haven't shot yet," he said. "I'm going to use a whole roll on the lunchroom. I want shots of the kids lining up with trays and of the ladies serving the food. What pictures are you going to take for the camera club?"

"I'm going to make some pictures of some tennis games after school," Hal said.

Tedson laughed. "I could have guessed that. That's all you ever take pictures of."

Hal didn't mind Tedson laughing. Maybe it would be fun to make pictures of something besides tennis games.

They were in front of the school now, and Hal saw Tony Scott talking to some kids by the front steps.

"Hi, Tony, Alice, Susan, Bill," Tedson called. He knew everyone in the school.

Hal didn't. He knew Susan because he had seen the red-headed girl play tennis. He thought Alice was in his English class, but he wasn't sure. He had seen Bill around the school, but he knew nothing about him.

Tedson and Hal joined the group. The talk was about a show the drama club was going to give the next week.

Hal hadn't heard about the program. It sounded as if it would be fun. Maybe he had been missing a lot of things because he spent all his time on the tennis courts.

He thought about tennis and the tournament. Tony seemed so sure he would win. Hal had not seen Tony play recently, and he wanted to see Tony in action so he could study his game.

He knew Tony thought Hal had been nasty when he refused his challenge the other day. Hal decided he could do something about that right now.

Hal called Tony to one side and asked, "Do you still want to play some tennis with me?"

Tony seemed surprised and said, "I

thought champions didn't want to play lowly beginners like me."

Hal winced. Maybe he deserved that. He had been high and mighty with Tony. At least, that's the way Tony looked at it.

"I just thought that it might be a good idea if we had a game before the tournament. You are going to want to practice, aren't you?"

"Sure," said Tony with a grin. "Why not? I'd like to play you. How about after school today?"

Now it was Hal's turn to be surprised.

"Don't you want to get in some practice before we play?" he asked.

Tony laughed. "Why?" he asked. "We're just playing for fun, aren't we?"

Hal smiled. If Tony thought it was just going to be a fun game, that was all right with him. "Fine," he said. "I'll see you at the courts after school."

"This is one game I want to see," said Tedson, who had overheard them. "It will be like a preview of the tournament."

"It's just a fun game," said Tony. "This one doesn't count. Only the tournament counts."

Hal didn't say anything. He wanted to win this fun game because that would prove that Tony was just another player Hal could beat.

After class, Hal rushed home to change clothes and get his racket and tennis balls.

"Take along a jacket," his mother said. "It looks like rain."

Hal didn't think about the weather as he hurried to the park. He had left his camera at home. He was not going to have time to take pictures this afternoon.

While he waited for a court to be free, Hal bounced a tennis ball with his racket. It was good practice.

Tedson and Susan arrived carrying raincoats.

"It smells like rain," Tedson said.

Hal glanced at the sky. There were some dark clouds. He was more concerned about the wind. A high wind could pick up a hit tennis ball and do strange things with it.

Tony came up to the small group.

"This new racket your father sold me feels good," he said. "Wouldn't it be funny if the first time I used the new racket I beat you?"

Tedson laughed. Hal forced a smile. He was not going to let Tony make him angry. He needed a cool head for tennis.

Some players left a court and Hal and Tony took it over and began to warm up. Hal had to admit that Tony's strokes were good. He didn't hurry his shots. He had control.

But could Tony keep control under the pressure of a game? Did he have power for the smashes? The game would furnish the answers.

"Ready to start?" Hal asked after a while.

"Sure," said Tony.

"Let's spin the racket for service," Hal said.

He twirled his racket and Tony called out, "Rough side."

The racket landed with the rough end of the strings up.

59

"I'll serve first," Tony said. "I guess luck is with me. Which side of the court do you want?"

"I'll take this side," Hal said. He was about to say that Tony would need more than luck, but he decided to be polite. "Good luck," he said.

Both boys took their positions. Tony went behind the baseline and bounced the ball a few times. Then he called out to Hal, "Ready?"

"Ready," Hal answered.

Tony tossed the ball up and his racket smashed down at the ball. It was a good serve that landed deep in the corner of the right court. Hal got his racket under the ball and knew it was going out of bounds. He was right.

"Fifteen-love," Tony called and smiled.

Tony had made the first point.

It was going to be his last point Hal told himself as he took his position for the next serve.

60

Hal was wrong. It wasn't Tony's last point. His next serve was a sizzler and Hal didn't even get a racket on it. It was an ace for Tony.

"Thirty-love," Tony called out, and Hal nodded. Tony had two points now and Hal had "love," which in tennis means zero.

Hal managed to return the next serve and that started a short rally. It ended when Tony drove the ball into the net.

Now Hal had a point and the score was 30-15.

Hal threw back his shoulders. That was more like it!

Tony's next serve hit the net and he served again. Hal drove the ball out of bounds. Another point for Tony.

"Forty-fifteen," Tony called.

If Tony could make another point now, he would win the game. But Hal thought he knew how to handle that hard driving service of Tony's. This time he hit the ball just after it had bounced on the ground and was about eight inches high. It was a half volley. Tony tried to kill the return and instead drove the ball out of bounds. Tony still needed only one more point to win the game.

Hal certainly wasn't about to give his opponent the point he needed. He looked up at Tony.

The other boy grinned. "I wasn't expecting that," he said.

Tony was having fun. Hal had been too busy trying to figure out Tony's service to notice before. To Tony it was just a fun game, and he was winning.

Tony served again, and Hal's return was good. They rallied, and Hal gained control of the exchange. He placed his shots so that Tony had to run from one side to the other to return the shots.

Finally a return passed Tony and he shrugged.

"You can't win them all," he said. "It's forty-all."

The game was tied up. Now either boy

could win by making two points in a row. Hal intended to do just that.

But Tony's serve was too hot to return and Tony called, "My advantage."

Tony now needed to take the next point to win. Hal had to take the next three points to win.

Hal returned the next serve and Tony's smash landed in the net.

"Deuce," Tony called. The game was tied up again.

Tony's next serve was a hammer blow that Hal couldn't handle.

"My ad," Tony called, and Hal nodded. Again, Tony needed only one point to win.

Hal returned the next service, and Tony sliced the ball. It skimmed the top of the net and dropped over.

"My game!" Tony called and grinned.

"Good game," Hal said. He wasn't just being polite. Tony had played a good game. "But it's only one game. To win the set you have to win six games. We change sides now and I serve. You won't be making many points on my service."

Tony looked up at the sky. "I think I felt some raindrops," he said. "Do you still want to play?"

Hal didn't bother looking up. "We should play at least one set," he said.

Tony shrugged. "OK," he said, "I'm ready."

Hal served. He had been working on his serve for years and it cut the right-hand corner. Tony didn't manage to get his racket on it. Nor did he handle the next serves. Hal won the game.

It was drizzling now, but the boys continued to play. Hal didn't even notice the raindrops. Tony served again and won that game. Hal served next and won his game.

It was two-all as they started the fifth game. It was 40-15 in Hal's favor when there was a clap of thunder and it seemed suddenly as if the clouds were being emptied of tons of rain. Both boys ran for the tennis

shed. Susan, Tedson, and everyone else on
the courts ran for the shed, too.

"That rain really came fast," said Tedson.
"Too bad your set was washed out."

"Sure," said Tony. He grinned. "I won two
games, and Hal won two games. I didn't do
badly for a beginner."

Hal had to admit Tony was right. "We didn't finish the set," he said. "I would have won it if we had played a full set."

Tony shrugged. "What's the difference? It was only a fun game. There were no real winners or losers."

Hal didn't say anything. He shivered as he listened to the rain beating on the roof of the shed. The fun game had counted. It had proved that Hal could lose.

6 Can't Win 'Em All

It was still raining when the Brock family sat down to supper.

"I love the sound of the rain against the windows," said Julie. "It's so romantic."

Mrs. Brock was spooning out the meat, potatoes, and vegetables onto each plate. She said, "I'm glad it rained today. My garden can use the moisture. I fertilized today, and the rain will be good for the ground."

"The rain spoiled my game today," Hal said glumly.

His father looked up. "Who were you playing? What happened?"

"I was playing Tony Scott," Hal said, "and we were in the fifth game of the set."

"And you were winning, of course," Julie said.

Hal didn't know whether his sister was teasing. It wasn't always easy to tell with Julie.

"You were winning?" his father asked, but the question almost sounded like a statement of fact.

Hal paused before answering. How could he explain to his father that Tony had won two games? Tony should not have won two games. He was only a beginner, while Hal had been playing all his life.

Hal wet his lips and swallowed before answering to give himself more time to think.

"Tony took two games," he said. "He has a wicked serve. It took me time to figure it out. I was winning the fifth game when the rain came down too hard to continue playing."

Hal expected his father to be annoyed, perhaps angry. After all, Hal was going to be a national champion. He could not lose games to boys who were really only beginners. He should not be losing to boys who didn't even take tennis seriously.

"That's good," Bo Brock said and smiled.

"Good?" Hal asked, not quite sure what his father meant.

"Yes, good," said his father. "You always play better against tough competition than you do against a pushover. Having Tony in the park tournament will make it very interesting."

"Yes," said Mrs. Brock. "I'm sure it will mean more to win against good players than against boys you have been beating for years."

"Is Tony that good?" Julie asked.

Hal shrugged. "He has a good serve. He's fast and doesn't get rattled. But this was only a fun game. I don't know how he'll play under the pressure of a tournament."

"He may win a game or two," Hal's father said. "But in the long stretch of a match, training will tell. You'll take him."

"Sure, I will," Hal said. "I can't lose to him."

"Would it be so terrible if you did lose?" Julie asked.

Hal looked at his sister. She wasn't teasing. How could she think there was even a possibility that he could lose? But Hal didn't get a chance to answer. His father was answering.

"Everyone loses now and then," Mr. Brock said. "It's not terrible if you lose to a better player. It's not even terrible if you lose to a player who isn't better than you. What counts is how losing affects you."

Hal looked at his father. They had never talked about losing before. They had always talked about winning.

"What do you mean, Dad?" Hal asked.

His father said, "You can lose if losing doesn't beat you. You've only lost a game, a match, or a set. It's all right as long as you aren't beaten."

Hal shook his head. He did not understand. "But if you lose, you are beaten." He glanced from his mother to his father.

"Look at it this way, Hal," his mother said. "When you were learning to ride a bicycle, you fell off a lot of times. But you weren't beaten. You climbed back onto the seat and tried again. And you learned to ride."

"Mom means you're beaten only if you quit because you lost," Julie said. "I lost a lot of tennis games, but I kept playing."

"You didn't lose that many games," her father said, smiling. "You still could make a very sweet woman's champ if you'd work at your game."

"No, thanks, Dad," laughed Julie. "One champion in the family is enough for me."

Mrs. Brock laughed, too. "Bo, if we'd let you, you'd have all of us, including me, on the tennis courts all the time, being trained to be champions."

Bo Brock nodded. "Well, Alice, I've always told you that you were a much better than average player. If you had only worked at it when you were young. . ."

Julie and her mother laughed again, and Hal joined in. After a moment, Mr. Brock chuckled, too.

The next morning, as usual, Hal and Tedson walked to school together. Both boys carried their cameras.

Hal expected Tedson would bring up the tennis game and how Tony had won two games. But Tedson had other things on his mind.

"Look, we have to have a series of pictures that tell a story for the camera club contest," he said. "I'm shooting my series on the school. Have you decided what your series will be?"

"I thought I'd take pictures of the tennis tournament," Hal said.

Tedson grinned. "I should have known! But how are you going to make pictures when you're playing in the tournament?"

Hal shrugged. "I'll find a way."

"Maybe you can string your camera around your neck, drop the racket, squeeze off a picture of your opponent serving the ball, then pick up your racket and hit the ball."

Hal laughed. "You're crazy! I couldn't play good tennis or make good pictures that way."

Tedson grinned. "Well, since winning at tennis is such a snap for you, I thought you might like to have something else to do when you're out on the court."

"After playing Tony yesterday, I figure I may be kept busy on the court just trying to win," Hal said. "I'm going to start my series this afternoon. I'll make a picture of the tournament schedule."

"I'll go with you," Tedson said. "You know, I'm in the tournament, too. I'm sure that will upset you because I'm difficult to beat."

Hal laughed. Only Tedson could make a joke out of losing.

Later, Hal handed his new theme to the English teacher.

Miss French glanced at it and said, "I'm happy to see you found something other than tennis to write about. I didn't know you were interested in photography."

"I like photography," said Hal, "but I'm not as good at it as Tedson."

"Tedson?" Miss French's right eyebrow arched. "Who is Tedson? Is he in my class?"

"Sure," Hal said. "That's Theodore Buris Junior. His mother calls his father Ted-dad and . . ."

"Tedson, son of Ted," Miss French finished and laughed. "Perhaps you could write a theme on how boys get nicknames."

"I'll remember," Hal said. He didn't have many ideas for themes when the teacher didn't assign a subject.

After classes, the boys went to the park

district tennis shack. The tournament schedule and draw was tacked to the door.

The draw named the boys who would play
each other in the first round.

"How lucky can I get?" Tedson asked with
a whistle after he studied the typewritten
list. "In the first round I play Joe DeLuga.
I'll never get to the second round."

"Don't think about losing," Hal said.
"You're as good a player as Joe DeLuga."

"If you want to have something to worry about," Tony said coming up to the group, "just remember that you may have to play me."

"Hi, Tony," Tedson greeted him. Hal wondered why Tedson didn't get angry at Tony's bragging, but Tedson didn't seem to mind.

"I plan on getting lucky," Tedson said. "I'll probably take the tournament away from both you and Hal."

"I'd like to see you do that," Tony said.

Hal laughed. It would be funny if Tedson somehow became the winner.

"I wouldn't mind," Hal said. "But I'm afraid it is going to take more than luck."

"You probably wouldn't mind losing to Tedson," Tony told Hal, "but you're not going to like losing to me."

"I don't expect to lose," Hal said.

"That's too bad," said Tony, "because I'm going to be the champion."

"That's fine, fellows," Coach Cohen said from the doorway of the tennis shack. "I like a spirited contest. But let's remember that tennis is a gentleman's game."

For a moment Hal had thought that he and Tony were headed for a fight, but Coach Cohen's words had changed all that.

Tedson grinned and said, "Neither of these two fellows has a chance to win. I'm taking this tournament with my secret weapon."

"What's your secret weapon?" Hal asked.

"An invisible ball," said Tedson. "If you can't see it, you can't return it."

Coach Milt Cohen joined in the laughter. "If the referee can't see the invisible ball, you're going to be in trouble."

Tedson waved his hand. "That's a small detail I'm working on."

Hal was snapping pictures of the schedule and draw tacked to the door.

Hal had checked to see who he was playing in the first round. It was Eddy Sulski. Hal had played him before and knew all his weaknesses.

Even as he snapped the pictures, Hal was thinking he would have to step up his training. He was sure to beat Eddy, but waiting would be Tony, and he wanted to be ready when he met Tony across a tennis net again.

7 Your Serve

Hal didn't take many pictures the rest of the week. He was too busy working out on the tennis courts with his father. After school, his father met him on the courts and served sizzling shots, one after the other, until Hal could handle them.

The only rest for Hal came when his father stepped to the net to discuss Hal's handling of the serve.

"That was better," Bo Brock said after an hour of practice. "Remember to make your move as soon as the ball leaves my racket. If you wait to see where the ball lands, you won't have time to get into position. You have to judge where the ball is going as soon as it is hit. I'll serve some more cannonballs. You know what to do?"

"Yes," said Hal. "I'll block and not try to drive. If you're rushing the net, I'll try for a low return. And if you're playing in the back-court, I'll try for a deep return or a short drop shot."

When he wasn't on the court or in school, Hal practiced against the garage wall behind his home. He kept working on his back-stroke, which he felt was weak.

Walking to school, Tedson said, "You'll tire yourself out before you play in the tour-nament. Meanwhile I'll be fresh because I have done no practicing, and I'll walk away with the tournament."

Hal grinned. Ted knew he didn't have a chance, but it didn't seem to bother him.

"How's your camera club picture series coming?" Tedson asked.

Hal shrugged. "I haven't had much time to snap pictures."

"I've printed up half of mine already," Tedson said. "Tony and I spent hours in the darkroom yesterday. He's learning fast."

Hal frowned. "Everything he tackles comes easy for him," he said.

"Don't kid yourself," said Tedson. "I'll tell you something. Tony makes everything look easy, but he works at it. He's working to learn darkroom technique, and he's working out on the tennis courts, too."

Hal found Tedson was right. That afternoon, while waiting for his father at the courts, he saw Tony working out with the coach.

Hal had his camera and snapped some pictures. The coach noticed Hal taking pictures and stepped off the court.

"I have to see somebody," he said. "Why don't you put that camera away and pick up a racket and give Tony some exercise?"

Hal shrugged. Why not? "Fine," he said.

But Tony wiped his forehead with the back of his hand. "I have had enough exercise for one day," he said. He grinned at Hal. "Besides, I don't need a lot of practice to win the tournament."

"You can never get enough practice," Coach Cohen said. And he hurried to the tennis shack.

"The coach is right," said Hal.

Tony smiled. "He's right for you tennis nuts who make a business of the game. But I'm in it for fun. And it will be fun taking the tournament championship."

Tony waved and left. Hal clenched his fists. Tony had a knack for making him angry without even trying.

He was still burning when his father came trotting out onto the courts. His playing was ragged. He knew he should be cool when he was playing. But somehow Hal kept thinking of Tony, and that made him angry and messed up his game.

Saturday morning was the day the tennis

tournament began, and Hal came to the courts early. He needed pictures for the camera club. He snapped some of the early arrivals as they rallied to get warm. He snapped pictures through the net as Tedson served some balls. He squeezed off some pictures to get Tedson as he rallied with another player.

Then Coach Cohen called all the players to the shack and read off the pairings and the court assignments for the first round of play. There were thirty-two players entered in the tournament. The winners of the sixteen games of the first round would be matched against each other in the second round.

The eight second-round winners would meet in the third round on Sunday morning. The four winners would play in the semi-finals that noon. Sometime Sunday afternoon the final match would be played, and the winner of the tournament would be decided.

Hal was paired with Eddy Sulski for the

first match. Eddy was a chunky boy who had a smashing drive but no speed.

They met and shook hands and spun the racket to decide who would serve first. Eddy won the spin.

"Just my luck," he said. "I hoped I'd play my first game against one of the other boys so I would have an even chance to win."

There was nothing Hal could say to make Eddy feel better. He liked Eddy, but it was just too bad he and Eddy were paired.

Eddy was nervous because he was playing against Hal. His first serve landed in the net. He foot faulted his second serve by stepping over the service line. With that bad beginning, he lost the first game quickly.

The boys changed sides, and Hal tried to calm Eddy down.

"Relax," Hal said. "You just had some bad breaks."

Eddy shrugged. He couldn't handle Hal's serve and didn't make a point in the second game.

Hal felt sorry for Eddy as they began the third game. He saw how miserable he felt at losing so badly. For the first time, Hal wondered how he would feel playing against a much better player. He'd probably feel as hopeless as Eddy did.

Eddy was serving. He was a bit calmer and did better, but he still lost.

Hal took the first set without losing a game. He won the second set and the match just as easily.

They shook hands after the last game and Eddy managed a grin. "I know I had to lose to you," he said, "but thanks for not making me feel like an idiot."

"Forget it," Hal said.

Hal reported his scores to Coach Cohen, who was standing by the bench entering the results on his clipboard.

Hal asked who he would play in the second round that afternoon. Coach Milton Cohen looked at his diagram on the clipboard and said Hal would play the winner of the match in court four.

Hal hoped he would meet Tony next. He wanted to get that match played and won. Then he could forget about Tony for the rest of the tournament.

Most of the first round matches were still

being played. Hal took more pictures, making sure he didn't get in anyone's way.

He watched Tony for a while. He was grinning as he smashed a return into the backcourt. The grin told Hal that Tony was winning.

Tedson came running up to Coach Cohen and saw Hal nearby with his camera.

"I won! I actually won!" Tedson shouted. "I've been playing against you so long that I forgot it was possible for me to win!"

"That's great!" Hal said. He was as excited as Tedson. He wanted his friend to win.

"I played Joe DeLuga and he must have had a bad day because I won!"

"Who do you play next?" Hal asked.

Tedson was still excited and he almost jumped up and down.

"Who do I play next?" he asked Coach Cohen. "I might even take this next match and then, with a lot of luck, I could end up in the semifinals and play you for the championship."

Coach Cohen was smiling at Tedson's excited happiness. He looked at his schedule and laughed.

"It seems that you were playing in court four," he told Tedson. "And since you won, your next match is against Hal Brock."

Tedson looked at the coach and his grin faded. Hal felt sorry. Tedson had been so happy winning, and now he would be playing Hal. Both boys knew that he never won against Hal.

Tedson shrugged and sighed. He managed to keep a small smile.

"Well," he said, "it was fun while it lasted."

Hal wanted his friend to feel good. "You could be lucky," he said.

"Lucky?" Tedson looked at Hal. "I don't need luck playing against you. I need a miracle."

After lunch, Hal returned to the courts. There were only eight matches now, and all the morning's losers were on the benches to watch the games.

Hal's father had wanted to come, but Saturday afternoons were busy ones at the shop.

Hal was relaxed for the match with Tedson. He knew what to expect, and he was happy when Tedson made a good play or won a point.

Tedson played a good game. He was much better than Eddy had been in the morning match. Hal had to work to win from Tedson. The first set was 7-5.

Tedson was tiring, and Hal won the second set, 6-3. He had won his second round match.

He and Tedson watched the other matches. Tony was playing a tall boy named Steve Janson. It was a seesaw battle. Tony finally won the last set, 9-7.

"You're a much better player than Steve," Tedson said. "You're a cinch to take Tony."

Hal wasn't so sure. Tony had had a tough game, but he had won. That was what counted. He won.

8 Rackets and Clubs

Before leaving the courts, Coach Cohen told Hal he would play Harry Davis in the morning. Hal went to his father's sports shop. He knew his father wanted to learn how the tournament was going.

His father was waiting on a customer when Hal entered the shop. His father looked up, and Hal made the OK sign with his finger and thumb to show he had won. His father smiled, and Hal wandered down the aisles. He stopped by the fishing section to admire the rods and to flip through some of the magazines.

He stopped at an advertisement for a sailboat. In the picture, the boy and girl were laughing as they leaned far out over the side to keep the small boat from tipping. It looked like fun.

Hal wanted to learn to sail someday. He had mentioned it to his father, but his dad had said there was not time to learn to sail and to train for the big time in tennis.

Hal moved on and ran his hand over an outboard motor. It looked powerful. He closed his eyes for a second and imagined himself pushing the motor to full speed and having the boat leap under him and cut through the water.

Tedson and his father went fishing often, and Tedson knew all about outboard motors. Tedson's father had asked Hal to go along on a fishing trip, but Hal had to refuse because he needed the time to work out on the tennis court.

There were a lot of customers in the store, and Hal noticed that his father and two salesmen were busy. Dropping his racket and a can of tennis balls behind the counter, Hal went up to a man in sports clothes who was drumming his fingers on the counter.

"May I help you?" Hal asked, smiling.

"Yes, you may," the man said. "I need some golf balls, and I'd like to look at some putters."

"Certainly, sir," Hal said, and led the way to the golfing items. Hal didn't know much about golf and could not recommend one brand of golf balls over another, but the man knew which brand he wanted.

"Which of these putters is the best?" the man asked, gripping a club.

"Golf isn't my game," Hal said, "but I'd pick the club that seems most comfortable to you. You don't want to be thinking about the club when you're putting. You just want to think of getting the ball into the hole."

The man chuckled. "You're right," he said. "If I were a good golfer, I suppose my old putter would be as good as a new one."

"Equipment is very important in any sport," Hal said. "A good player needs good equipment."

The customer laughed. "You're quite a salesman for a youngster," he said. He tried several clubs and selected one.

Hal returned to the counter to wrap the purchases, figure out the bill, and write a receipt.

"Thank you," Hal said, and the man waved as he walked out. Hal kept smiling.

No one had told him he was a good salesman before. He waited on customers once in a while, but he had never wondered if he was a good salesman. It was nice to know he did something well besides tennis.

Hal waited on several customers and lost track of time as he became interested in trying to help each person with his selection. He thanked a woman who had bought some fishing lures and looked up to see only a stray shopper or two in the store.

Jimmy, who had been a salesman in the

sports shop ever since Hal could remember, patted him on the shoulder.

"Nice going, Hal," he said. "You really helped us out a lot. You did a nice job of selling. I watched and was very proud of you."

"Thanks," Hal grinned. "I didn't do anything special."

"Maybe not," Jimmy said, "but you didn't do anything wrong. You sent your customers away happy, and they'll come back."

Hal didn't know what he had done that was so good, but he was glad to hear the praise. No one before, it seemed to Hal, had praised him for anything but the way he played tennis.

"I can't wait to hear about the tournament," his father said, turning to Hal. "How did it go?"

"I won my first and second round matches," Hal said. "There's a third round tomorrow morning and if I win, there's the semifinals and the finals."

"You'll win," his father said. "Do you know

who you're likely to play in the semifinals and the finals? You want to study their games and think through their tactics tonight so you will be ready for them tomorrow."

"I suppose so," Hal said.

"You ought to be on top of the world right now," Jimmy said. "You just won two matches. Are you going to celebrate?"

Hal shook his head. He didn't feel like celebrating. Winning was nothing special to him. Losing would be terrible, but winning was just something he took in stride.

"There's time for celebrating after we win the final match," Bo Brock said.

Hal noticed his father said "we" even though Hal would be playing the games. Winning the tournament meant a lot to his father.

"I'm tired," Hal said. "I'd like to forget tennis for a while."

His father nodded. "Of course you're tired. You'll feel better after we have supper. But we can't forget tennis now. Tonight you have

96

to think over your strategy. That's how championships are won."

"I have homework to do tonight," Hal said. "I don't want to have to worry about getting it done tomorrow."

His father looked at him. "I'm not going to force you to think through how you're going to play tomorrow," he said. "But a champion thinks ahead and prepares. He doesn't wait until he gets to the courts to work out his strategy. It's up to you if you want to be just another good player or a champion. Let's close up here and get home to supper."

At the supper table, Julie said she was happy that he had won today. "But you don't mind if I don't come out to see you win the championship tomorrow, do you?" she asked. "Susie's mother is taking some of us girls out to the country for a picnic."

"Don't you think it's important to be there to see your brother win an important tournament?" Mr. Brock asked, frowning.

"I don't mind," Hal said. "I'll be too busy to notice if you're there or not."

"You go and have fun, Julie," Mrs. Brock said. "Your father and I will be there, and we'll give you a play-by-play account of what happens."

Julie smiled. "I'm proud of my brother, but I've seen him play tennis before. In fact, I remember beating him a few times."

Hal grinned. "You sure did. You're a wicked tennis player."

"He was much younger then," their father said. "Julie, you couldn't beat him now."

They rose from the table and Mr. Brock asked Hal, "Do you want to discuss strategy now?"

"Well, I do have homework . . ."

"Homework first," Hal's mother said as she and Julie cleared the table. "Whether he wins or loses tomorrow, he still has to have his homework ready for class Monday morning."

"Of course," Mr. Brock said. "I know that

tennis is just a game to some people in this family. I'll be ready to talk tactics any time you want to, Hal."

In his room, Hal spread his books on the desk and tried to think about the homework assignments.

He himself didn't understand why he didn't want to think about the games tomorrow. He was tired, but he had been tired before and still had been eager to discuss the details of the game.

Hal knew his father was right. If he wanted to win the tournament, he should be thinking of what problems he might be faced with on the courts tomorrow. He was a good tennis player because he worked at it and studied. He wasn't like Tony. Tony could do a lot of things well without a lot of work, or so it seemed anyway.

But Hal knew he wasn't Tony. He wasn't a star at school or in photography or at anything but tennis.

Still, just this afternoon at the store,

Jimmy had said he was a good salesman. Hal smiled remembering the praise.

Maybe if he put in the time and study on other things, he could be as good at them as he was at tennis. He hadn't thought about it before.

He did his homework slowly and carefully. The work wasn't difficult. It should not be too hard to become a really good student, Hal thought.

He finished the assignment and put his books away.

He knew his father was waiting to talk about the tournament matches to be played tomorrow. Hal would not disappoint his father. He would discuss strategy with him.

But Hal wished that just once he could be like Tony and play the game for the fun of it.

9 Tournament Play

Sunday morning, Hal and his father went to the courts. Hal's mother said she would come out to the courts later.

Only four tennis courts were needed for the tournament this morning.

"Pace yourself," Mr. Brock said as Hal shrugged out of his sweater. "Remember, you have three matches to win today."

Hal nodded. "Coach Cohen says if the players are tired, he may put off the final match to Monday afternoon."

But before the final match there were two other matches. Hal had to win them both if he was to play for the championship.

His third round opponent was Harry Red Davis. He was a tall boy who played on the high school football team.

The boys rallied until they were ready to start the game. They shook hands at the net.

Red had won the serve. He had a lot of power, and he used it. His serves were torpedoes Hal could not return.

Hal wasn't upset. He knew the big boy couldn't keep up the power play. He would get tired, and then Hal would take command.

Red won the first game on his serves. The boys changed courts, and now Hal served. He worked his shots carefully, placing them to make Red do a lot of chasing.

Red began to get winded and lose control. His smashes went out of bounds. His serves lost their sizzle.

Hal won the first set, 7-5. Hal continued

his careful game, and Red's power melted away. Hal won the second set easily, 6-2. He had won his third-round match.

The boys shook hands after the match, and Hal almost felt sorry for Red.

The older boy just shrugged. "Now I know why they say you're going to be a champion," he said.

Hal had a chance to rest between matches. He had played only two sets while some of the other matches had gone into third sets.

His father was waiting for him at the bench. "You played him well," Mr. Brock said. "Now watch Tony's style. You may meet him in the next match, and you have to win that one to play in the final."

Hal nodded. He had just won a match, but it didn't count. What counted were the matches left to play. He recalled something Coach Milt Cohen had once said about championship play. There was always one more game to play and to win. You never finished.

Hal glanced around and saw Tedson near the fence with some kids. They seemed to be having fun. They could take tennis or leave it.

Then he studied the game. Only four players were left when the third round finished. Hal, Tony Scott, Skinny Loftus, and Randy Kemm.

Hal wanted to play Tony next. He wanted to be fresh for the match with Tony. It was more important to win over Tony than to win the tournament. Tony put on such an air of being able to do anything without having to work at it. More than anything, Hal wanted to wipe that grin of victory from Tony's face.

But Coach Cohen said Hal drew Skinny Loftus for the semifinal round. Tony was playing Randy Kemm.

Hal tried to remember everything he knew about Skinny as they spun the racket to see who served first. Hal had to get through this match in order to play Tony, who he was sure would win his match with Randy.

The boys shook hands, and Skinny smiled and said quietly, "This is going to be an interesting match."

Skinny was right. It was an interesting match. Skinny was not tall, and he was thin, but he was far from weak. He did as much planning as Hal did. In fact, both boys played the same kind of game.

Hal grinned as he saw Skinny placing his shots so that Hal would wear himself out running. It was smart tennis. He had done the same thing when playing Red. Hal forgot about Tony and concentrated on out-thinking Skinny Loftus.

It was a tight battle all the way. The first set went twenty-two games before Hal won 12-10.

Hal changed his style for the second set. He put on a power play when serving and then switched to careful placement when Skinny served. The tactic worked. Hal won the second set and the match, 8-6.

Skinny was panting and his face was damp with sweat as they shook hands.

Hal was breathing hard, too.

"You really play tennis," Hal said. "You play my kind of game."

"I know," Skinny grinned. "I've been studying your game and I copied it."

Hal didn't know what to say. Imagine, someone had thought he was good enough to copy his style!

Then Coach Cohen was there and reporting that Tony had won his match.

"Both you and Tony have played a lot of tennis today," the coach said. "We can play the final match tomorrow afternoon. Or if you like, we can take a break for a few hours so you can eat and rest and decide the championship this afternoon."

Tony Scott grinned. "I'm fresh as a daisy," he said. "Let's finish it off this afternoon."

Hal was tired, but he wasn't going to admit it to Tony.

"This afternoon is fine with me," he said.

His father and mother were waiting to drive him home.

"You must be exhausted," his mother said. "We'll have a light lunch, and you'll take a nap."

"I've been studying Tony's game," Hal's father said. "I think he has a couple of weaknesses you can play on."

Hal didn't say anything. He was still thinking of that match with Skinny. He was very proud of having won that match, but his father wasn't even mentioning it. He was thinking about the game he would play against Tony Scott.

After lunch, Hal's mother insisted he go to his room and stretch out on the bed. Hal said he couldn't sleep in the daytime, but he did.

All too soon his father was shaking him awake and they drove back to the tennis courts.

"I'll win this one for you, Dad," Hal said.

"No," said his mother. "Win it for yourself

because it's what you want to do."

Hal thought about the remark, but then he and Tony were watching Coach Cohen spin the racket. Tony called "rough" and the rough side came up. He had won the serve.

Coach Cohen walked off the court, and Tony said, "I want to thank you, Hal, for getting me this far in the tournament."

Hal was surprised and did not understand. He had done nothing to help Tony.

"You made me so angry saying I had no right to enter the tournament that I made it my business to win," said Tony. "And here we are!"

Hal had been angry with Tony because of his bragging. Now he realized that Tony had his own reasons for being angry with Hal.

"Yes, here we are!" Hal said.

Hal had called Tony a beginner. Some beginner! Tony had won as many matches as Hal.

They rallied for a few minutes and then Tony called "Ready?" and Hal nodded.

Tony served, and the championship match was on.

Hal tensed waiting for the ball to bounce. It landed on the marker and Hal knew he couldn't get to it in time.

The coach looked at Hal.

"In or out?" Coach Cohen asked.

"In," Hal said quietly.

Coach Cohen nodded. "That's what I thought too, but I wasn't sure."

"Fifteen-love," Tony called. He had made the first point. He served again and Hal's return was out of bounds.

"Thirty-love."

"Relax," Hal told himself. Tony was just another player. He was no one to frighten him. He was only a beginner.

But Hal didn't relax, and he lost the first game.

Now it was his turn to serve. But Tony returned Hal's serves without any trouble.

Tony grinned and won the second game.

That grin made Hal angry. He promised

himself that Tony wouldn't win another game. But Tony did.

He won three straight games, and Hal had won one.

They changed courts, and Hal was fuming. He was being beaten by an amateur, a beginner! He couldn't believe it.

He was angry, and he played badly and that made him more angry. He knew the worst thing a tennis player can do is to get angry. You can't think straight.

Hal tried to calm down. After all, Tony had a right to enter the tournament. Anyone who wanted to enter had a right to do so. So why was he angry?

Because Tony seemed to win without working at it. He just grinned and had a good time.

Well, Hal told himself, there was no rule against that!

Tony was a good player. He was proving it by beating Hal.

Hal's anger dripped away. He forgot the other player was named Tony Scott, a beginner who could win without trying.

Hal's playing improved. His control came back. He sent smashing serves which Tony couldn't return. And he won the game.

Hal thought only of the game now. He forgot about Tony and the crowd and thought only of where he wanted the next ball to land. He won three straight games, and the match was even at three-all.

Tony didn't quit. He played well. His overhead smashes had power behind them. His placements were accurate.

Hal felt himself getting tired. The long first set with Skinny had used up a lot of his strength. Now Hal's smashes had lost some of their sting.

The set was at six-all and then Tony won the next game. Hal fought back to win the next game to make the set seven-all. Tony took the next game, and then Hal misjudged a forehand and the ball hit the net. Tony had won the game and the set, 9-7.

Hal had lost the first set! All Tony had to do to win the championship was win another set. But Hal had to win the next two sets. And he was tired.

And for the first time in his life, Hal knew he was going to lose!

10 Winner and Champion

Tony was grinning as they changed courts.

"Meet the new champion," Tony laughed.

Hal was too tired to get angry. Tony was right. He was going to be the new champion. But Hal could not quit. He remembered his father saying you could lose without being beaten.

Well, he wasn't going to be beaten. After all, he had not lost yet. All he needed to do was win the next two sets!

"As I understand the rules," Hal said quietly, "the winner has to take two out of three sets."

"That's right," Tony said brightly. "I think I have a good chance to win one of the next two sets. Do you think you can stop me?"

Hal grinned. "I'm going to try," he said. "I'm going to try."

They played. Hal was being very careful now. He watched Tony's feet because sometimes a player's stance gives a hint of where the ball is being hit. He played each stroke as if it were the most important in the tournament.

Hal knew that many people were watching the match because every so often he was aware of applause when he or Tony made a good overhead smash or stroked a drop shot which just cleared the net. But he didn't think about the crowd. He thought about Tony and the game.

Tony wasn't taking chances either. He was playing as careful a game as Hal. Many of the games went to deuce and advantage and back to deuce and seesawed until it seemed almost luck when one of the boys made two points in a row and won the game.

Both boys were playing hard and were hot and tired.

The set was tied at eleven-all. Hal arched his back and stretched to get the knots out of his neck muscles. He served to Tony's backhand. Tony was off his stride and his return lob went out of bounds.

"Fifteen-love," Hal called.

He had to win this game, he told himself, and he used every bit of power he had left to send in stinging serves. They did the trick. He won the game and the set.

Now he and Tony were even. The next set would decide which boy was champion.

"Ten minutes rest," Coach Cohen called and Hal was happy to hear the words. He needed the rest.

His family and Tedson were waiting at the bench. His mother handed him a damp towel and Tedson had water which Hal sipped.

"You look worn out," Hal's mother said.

"I am kind of tired," Hal said.

116

"Both you and Tony look ready to drop," said Tedson, "but that's some tennis match!"

"Here, twist around on the bench and I'll massage your neck," Hal's father said. Hal turned and his father's big hands started kneading his shoulder and neck. It felt wonderful.

"I know how your muscles can knot up," Bo Brock said. "You have played a lot of tennis today. This final match should have been played later in the week."

"Coach Cohen suggested that," Hal said, "but Tony was eager to play it today and I didn't want to sound like it mattered, so I agreed."

His father's fingers still were rubbing the sore muscles of his neck and shoulders.

"Tony has to be just as tired as you are," his father said.

"I don't know," said Hal. "I had that long drawn-out match with Skinny Loftus. And Tony seems to be having a lot of fun playing this match."

"Aren't you?" his father asked. "It's been an exciting tournament."

Hal thought about his father's question as he walked out onto the court to begin the third and last set. Tony was rubbing the back of his neck as he walked onto the court.

"I don't know about you," Tony said, "but I'm pooped."

Hal had never expected Tony to admit that he was tired or that anything was difficult for him.

"I thought this was a breeze for you," Hal said.

Tony laughed. "I wouldn't call playing against you a breeze. It's more like going through a hurricane. Shall we get on with it, Champ?"

Hal smiled. Tony's teasing would have annoyed him at one time but now it didn't bother him. Tony was all right and he was a darn good tennis player.

"OK, Champ," Hal said.

He served and then the action was too

118

fast to do any thinking except where the ball was going to land next.

Hal wasn't thinking now about winning the tournament or losing it. Once he had admitted to himself he could lose, he no longer felt tensed up. Now he could enjoy the give and take of the game.

As they changed courts, Tony said, "You must have your second wind. I had you chasing those balls pretty good on that last rally."

"I'm getting less tired by the minute," Hal laughed. "How about you?"

Tony grinned. "I'll last just as long as you do, Champ."

The match was fairly even. Neither boy was ever more than one game ahead of the other.

In the twelfth game, Tony was leading 6-5.

Tony was serving and the score was 40-30, in Tony's favor.

Tony served and Hal sliced the return. The ball sailed just over the net and dropped, bounced and Tony missed it.

"Deuce," Tony called. The game was tied up.

His next serve was a sizzler which landed on the marker, and Hal couldn't play it.

"Good," Hal said as he waved his hand in the safe sign.

"My advantage," Tony said. He grinned. "You're about to lose, Champ."

Hal returned the grin. He wasn't worried. It was a fun game.

Tony's next serve cleared the net and Hal sliced the ball but this time Tony was set and lobbed a return. Hal resisted the temptation to smash it for fear the ball would go wild. He took an easy forehand stroke.

They rallied. They played deep and they played each stroke with sure hands.

Then Tony sliced the ball and Hal raced to the net, reaching it just in time to see the ball ripple the tape and dribble away.

It was Tony's point. It was game point. And match point.

120

Tony was the winner! He was the champion now.

Hal had lost!

Tony held his hand out at the net and Hal shook it.

"Congratulations!" Hal said and his voice sounded dry and scratchy to his ears.

"Thanks, Champ," Tony said.

"You're the champ now," Hal said. "You know, I feel good!"

"But you just lost the tournament," said Tony. "I bet it's the first time you ever lost an important match."

Hal grinned. "It is the first time and I always worried what it would feel like to lose. Now that it has happened, it doesn't feel so terrible."

Tony grinned. "I'll let you in on a secret too," he said. "I wanted to beat you so bad that I thought winning would be just great. But now that I've won a match from you, I don't feel anything special!"

Then Coach Cohen was running toward

them and smiling. He put an arm over both their shoulders.

"Great tennis!" he chuckled. "We have medallions for the winner and runner-up."

Hal looked for his father as he saw the crowd rushing in to watch the presentation ceremony. But Hal only saw a blur of faces.

There were no long speeches at the award ceremony.

Coach Cohen handed each boy his medallion. Tony's was gold and said "Winner," and Hal's was silver and said "Second Place."

Tedson broke out of the crowd and shook Hal's hand.

"You lost like a champion," he said.

Hal laughed. "Losing wasn't hard to do."

But seeing his father after he lost would be hard to do. Bo Brock had counted so on his winning. After all a future champion could not lose a little park tournament.

Some boys and girls came up to Hal and they said they were sorry he lost.

A stocky man with glasses came up to Hal

122

and said, "I'm Tony's father and I just wanted to say that now I can understand why Tony trained so hard. You are a very good tennis player."

Hal stared at Mr. Scott. "Tony trained hard? I thought everything came easy to Tony."

His father laughed. "He learns quickly but he works at it. He was out on the court every morning before school hours. He bounced a tennis ball against the garage door until bed-time. Don't let him kid you. He trained."

Hal grinned. "Thanks, Mr. Scott," he said. "That's the best news I've had today."

Hal's parents were waiting for him. His mother admired the silver medallion and his father slapped him on the back and said, "Well played."

"But I lost," Hal said.

His father nodded.

Hal looked at his father and knew how much his father wanted him to be a tennis champion. Hal glanced at the courts where

Tony was posing for a picture with his medallion.

"Dad," said Hal, "I lost and I'm not even sorry. I know I should be, because champions aren't supposed to lose. But right now, all I want to do is get my camera and make a picture of Tony for my camera club series. I mean, I don't want to be a tennis champion more than anything else in the world. I've been missing out on a lot of fun in school because all I did was play tennis. I want to find out about all the things I've been missing."

Hal held his breath. He had not known he was going to say all that to his father. How must his father feel now?

All Bo Brock said was, "Your camera is on the bench. Go get your picture."

Hal ran for the camera and posed Tony at the net with his racket. It would be the last picture in his series for the camera club. He had the title for the picture, "Winner and Champion."

Hal returned to his parents. He didn't

know what to say to his father.

"Don't worry, Hal," his father said. "You're not the first champion who lost a match. I think you can take Tony if you play again."

"So do I," said Hal. And he grinned. Because he knew it wouldn't really matter whether he won his next game with Tony. It would just be fun playing tennis.

MIKE NEIGOFF

A Chicagoan, Mike Neigoff began his university work at Northwestern, majoring in sociology. Four years in the infantry in World War II intervened, and when Mike returned he changed his field to journalism. After graduation, Mike worked on several newspapers in and around Chicago. Coming to television news work by way of radio, Mike was seen as a reporter on regular shows on two of the major television network stations in Chicago.

Commitment to improving the quality of city living led Mike into a new career in public relations for the redevelopment of Chicago neighborhoods. He is presently general assistant to the public relations director for the City of Chicago. Fortunately, sailing on Lake Michigan proves a good foil to this challenging work.

Writing, too, is a change of pace for Mike. His pleasure comes in telling stories "that people, big or little, take time to read and enjoy." Boys find Mike's sports stories fast paced, accurate, and easy to read.